Going to a Wedding

We have one big bag
and two small bags.
And we have a red
water bottle.

The train has not yet come. Many people are coming.
They are all waiting for the train. Where is the rest of the family?

There! I can see my grandfather. He is walking slowly.
He is looking for us.
My grandmother is behind him.

"Wait," says my mother. "We are not even on the train. I have sweets if you are hungry. I have water if you are thirsty. But wait till the train comes."

My grandfather has a very small bag.
He also has a stick.
My grandmother's bag is big.
I think there are many good things to eat in it.

My fat aunt has arrived. Her thin husband is here too. Their suitcase is full of clothes. They both like to dress up.

There is a big noise. The train is coming. The train is coming!
Everyone wants to get in. Where is the young man, who is getting married? We are all ready. But where is he? My father goes to look for my uncle. My grandfather looks too.

My mother looks worried. But my grandmother is smiling. "There he is!" grandmother says.
My uncle is running towards us. "So sorry, so sorry," he says. We all get on the train. The train leaves the station.

Printed in Great Britain
by Amazon

27451375R00016